The Sleeping Beauty

Story by:
Wilhelm and Jacob Grimm

Adapted by:
Margaret Ann Hughes

Illustrated by:
Russell Hicks
Douglas McCarthy
Theresa Mazurek
Allyn Conley-Gorniak
Julie Ann Armstrong

This Book Belongs To:

Use this symbol to match book and cassette.

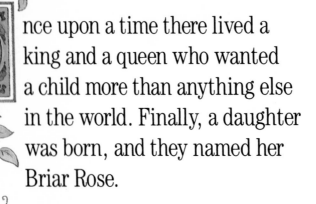

nce upon a time there lived a
king and a queen who wanted
a child more than anything else
in the world. Finally, a daughter
was born, and they named her
Briar Rose.

Now to celebrate the birth of
the princess, the king and queen
invited everyone in the kingdom
to a party, including seven
kind fairies.

After much eating and dancing,
it was time to give gifts to the
baby princess, Briar Rose.
The seven fairies came forward,
one at a time, and gave very
special gifts.

The first six fairies gave the gifts of beauty, music, honesty, bravery, grace and a loving heart. The seventh and last fairy, Belinda, was about to give her gift when…the room filled with whirling light and smoke. There suddenly appeared…another fairy! Her name was Faruza.

Faruza wasn't pleased at having been forgotten. In fact, she was quite angry.

She approached the sleeping baby and gave her gift…On her sixteenth birthday, Briar Rose would prick her finger on the spindle of a spinning wheel…and die.

Then, with a whirl of black smoke, Faruza disappeared.

Everyone was quite upset, and they didn't know what to do, when Belinda stepped forward.

She could not take away Faruza's evil gift of death entirely, but she could change it to sleep–a sleep that would fall upon the entire castle until the princess could be awakened by a kiss from a courageous prince.

Immediately the king ordered that all spinning wheels in the kingdom be destroyed.

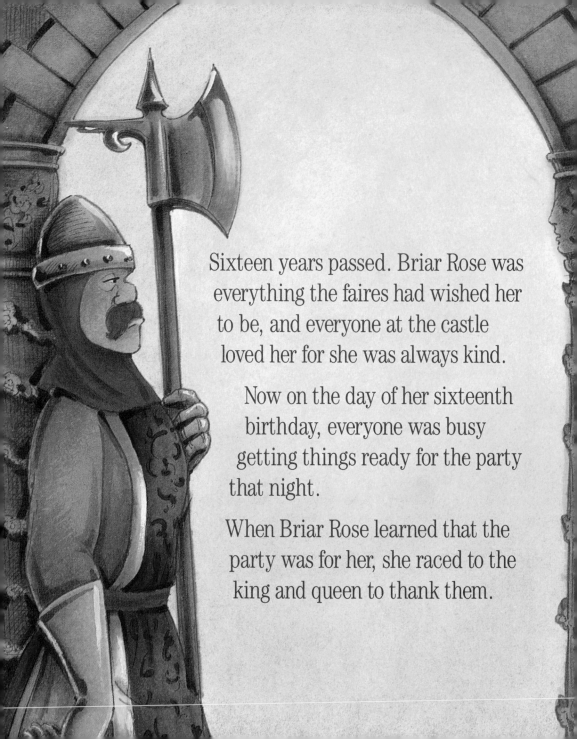

Sixteen years passed. Briar Rose was everything the faires had wished her to be, and everyone at the castle loved her for she was always kind.

Now on the day of her sixteenth birthday, everyone was busy getting things ready for the party that night.

When Briar Rose learned that the party was for her, she raced to the king and queen to thank them.

Oh, it was a happy birthday, indeed! The spell
of the angry Faruza had been broken! Briar Rose
and the prince were married, and the seven kind
fairies came to the wedding. No one ever discovered
that it was Grizzle's test of courage that helped the
prince succeed, and that Grizzle was really Belinda,
all along.

And when your dream has happened,
It will seem to others watching
That your dream has simply happened
In the twinkling of an eye.

 nd they all lived
happily ever after.

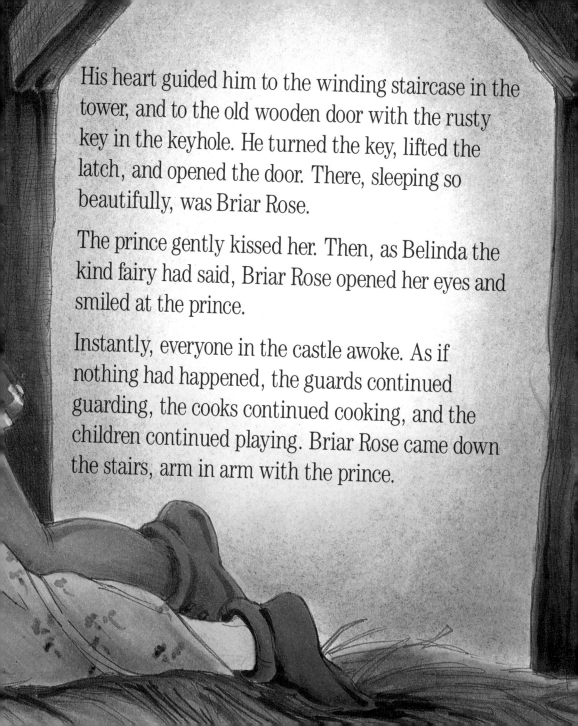

His heart guided him to the winding staircase in the tower, and to the old wooden door with the rusty key in the keyhole. He turned the key, lifted the latch, and opened the door. There, sleeping so beautifully, was Briar Rose.

The prince gently kissed her. Then, as Belinda the kind fairy had said, Briar Rose opened her eyes and smiled at the prince.

Instantly, everyone in the castle awoke. As if nothing had happened, the guards continued guarding, the cooks continued cooking, and the children continued playing. Briar Rose came down the stairs, arm in arm with the prince.

The thorns were strong, but so was the prince. Swinging his sword and making every blow count, the prince swung his sword again and again. The thorns tore at his clothes, but he didn't give up... until, he hit a very large branch, and...

He found the door to the castle. As he touched the door, it magically opened before him, and he stepped inside. All around him the prince saw everyone sleeping.

With that, the prince mounted his horse and rode quickly to the castle. Grizzle had made him even more determined. He pulled out his sword and swung at every branch that stood between him and the dream of his princess.

News of the sleeping princess spread throughout the country. Many young princes tried to cut through the thorny wall to get to her, but the thorns were sharp, and the branches were thick. Everyone who tried, failed.

Then one day, a young prince came from a distant land to rescue the princess. Cold and tired, he spied a campfire in the forest just outside the castle. There he met a strange little man, who had been keeping watch over the castle for many long years. His name was Grizzle.

The two shared the fire, and the prince asked Grizzle about the sleeping princess.

The prince was certain he could rescue Briar Rose, but Grizzle would not believe him, and he kept shaking his head.

To prevent anyone from rescuing the princess, Faruza magically placed a thick wall of giant rose bushes with very sharp thorns all around the castle, making it impossible to get inside…and no one ever did! The castle remained totally quiet, behind its wall of thorns, for a very long time.

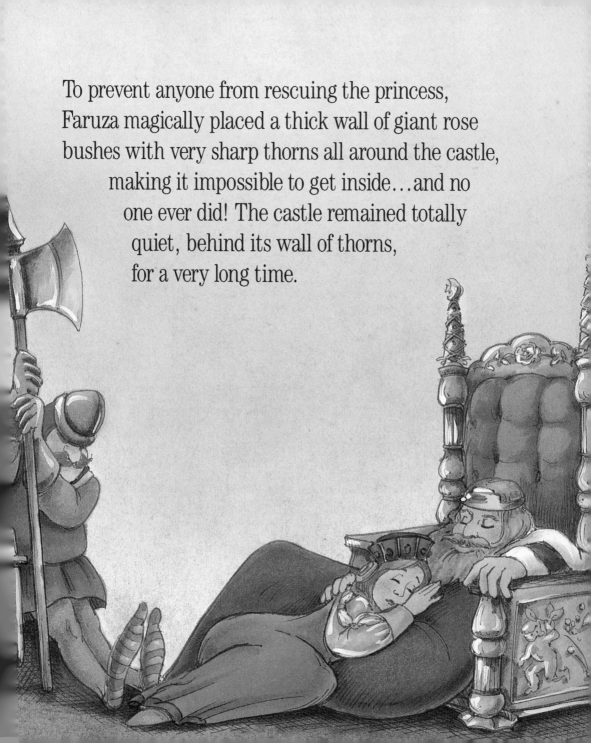

As Faruza vanished, a sleep gently fell over the castle, as in Belinda's wish. The guards stopped guarding, the cooks stopped cooking, and the children stopped playing. Everyone fell fast asleep– even the king and queen.

There sat an old woman next to an old machine with a large wheel at one end.

Briar Rose approached the old woman and reached out to touch the machine. It was a spinning wheel, and as she touched it, she pricked her finger on the spindle, and...

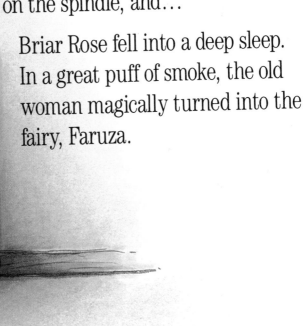

Briar Rose fell into a deep sleep. In a great puff of smoke, the old woman magically turned into the fairy, Faruza.

No princess could have been happier
that day. As the king and queen made
party plans, Briar Rose wandered
about the castle. In the courtyard she
found an unusual tower that she had
never seen before.

She climbed the old winding staircase
within the tower–up, up, up to the top.
At the top of the stairs was an old wooden
door with a rusty key in the keyhole.
She turned the key, lifted the latch,
and went inside the room.